Slow
Samson

SAMSON'S BRANCH

MAC'S HOLLOW

TERRY'S TREE

ARNOLD'S
BURROW

THE PARTY
PLACE

LIZZ'S
LOG

COCO'S
CANOPY

To Helen, Chris, Katie and Olivia, thank you for everything!

A TEMPLAR BOOK

First published in the UK in 2019 by Templar Publishing,
an imprint of Kings Road Publishing, part of Bonnier Books UK,
The Plaza, 535 King's Road, London, SW10 0SZ
www.templarco.co.uk
www.bonnierbooks.co.uk

1 3 5 7 9 10 8 6 4 2

ISBN 978-1-78370-855-0 (hardback)
ISBN 978-1-78370-870-3 (paperback)

This book was typeset in Trocchi
The illustrations were created with gouache paint,
coloured pencils and digital painting

Edited by Katie Haworth
Designed by Olivia Cook

Printed in China

Slow Samson

Bethany Christou

templar
books

The thing that Samson the sloth
loved more than anything in the world
was to make others happy.

Samson had lots of friends
and got invited to lots of parties,
but there was one problem . . .

Samson was
slow.

Hey,
Samson!

Hi,
Fran!

While he climbed through the trees
and chatted to a tree frog . . .

HAPPY BIRTHDAY TERRY!

the party
was starting.

While Samson stopped to sort out an argument . . .

his friends danced the conga.

And while he helped a toppled tortoise . . .

Take care!

his friends sang 'Happy Birthday'.

By the time Samson finally
arrived, the cake was all gone
and the party had finished.

HAPPY BIRTHDAY TERRY!

He had missed everything!

"Oh no!" thought Samson.

"It's because I got distracted along the way.

Next time I'm going to **hurry.**"

On his way to the next party, Samson didn't stop for the tree frog.

Sorry, got to rush.

Work it out yourselves.

He had no time for the monkeys.

And he charged past the tortoise.

Can't stop!

And if anyone asked for help,
Samson said . . .

He was out of breath
when he arrived . . .

but even at top speed he was
still slow.

He'd been horrible and rude to everyone for nothing!

Without Samson stopping to help, everything had gone wrong.

The tortoise had spent the
whole day stuck on his back.

The tree frog had
no one to talk to.

And the monkeys' arguing had annoyed the whole rainforest.

"I'm just so slow," Samson sobbed.

"No matter what I do, I'll never
make it to a party on time."

Samson's friends were worried about him.

"We need a plan!" said Mac.

Ideas

Together they came up with
lots of different ideas . . .

rocket pack!

oops

CRASH!

balloons?

can't
control

?

?

invite

rollerskates?

sloths
can't
stand...

catapult
him?

and one seemed
like it might just work.

The next day, Samson received a new invitation.

He knew he would be late again, but his friends were looking forward to seeing him.

He couldn't let them down.

Samson set off for the party. This time he didn't hurry.

He stopped to chat
to the tree frog.

Hey,
Fran.

Not
now...

Gotta
dash!

And he was ready to
help the monkeys . . .

Gotta
go!

and the tortoise.

Can't
stop now...

But they all rushed off when they saw him.
"They must be very mad at me," thought Samson.

Samson felt
awfully lonely.

And he was
still slow.

By the time Samson arrived
he was sure he was hours late.

But to his surprise he found . . .

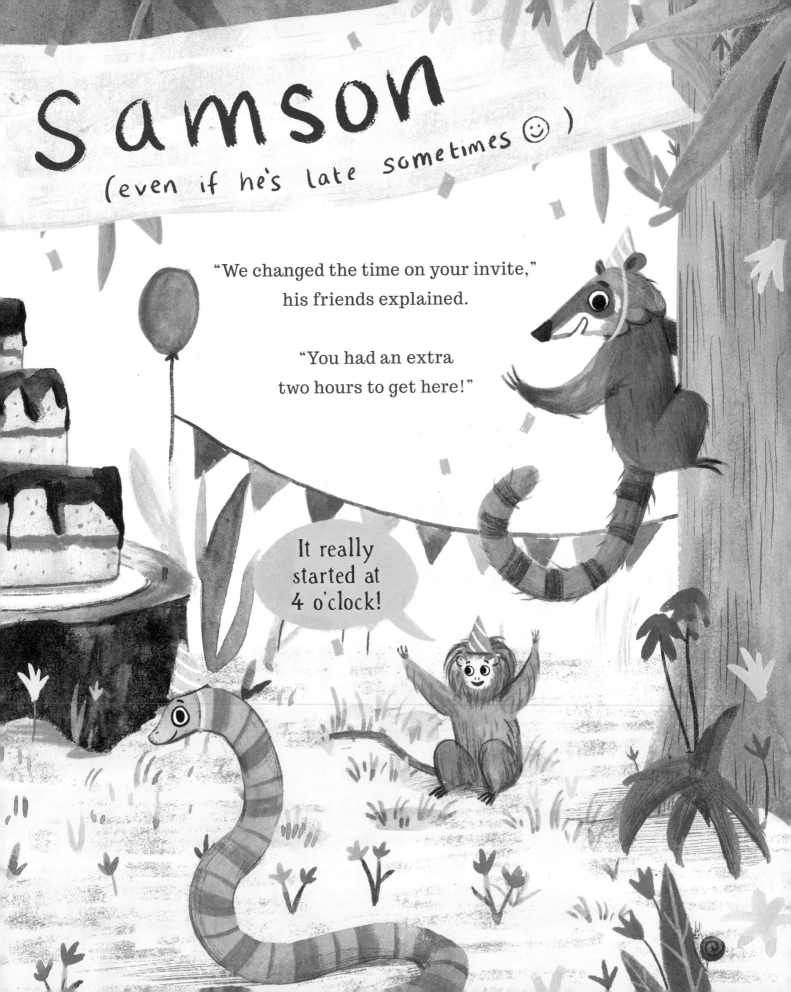

There was dancing,
there were party games . . .

and there was **plenty** of cake!

But best of all . . .

Best day!

. . . Samson had an amazing time
with his friends!

SAMSON

Thanks for
drawing us!

So funny!

Everyone agreed that it was the best party yet,
because Samson had been there to share it with them.

ARNOLD'S
BURROW

THE PARTY
PLACE

LIZZ'S
LOG

COCO'S
CANOPY

More Picture Books from Templar:

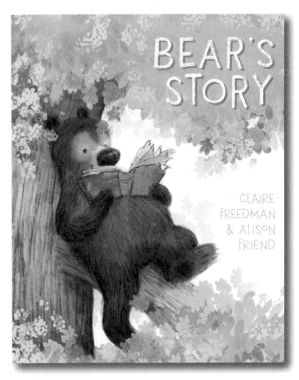

ISBN: 978-1-78370-644-0

ISBN: 978-1-78741-234-7

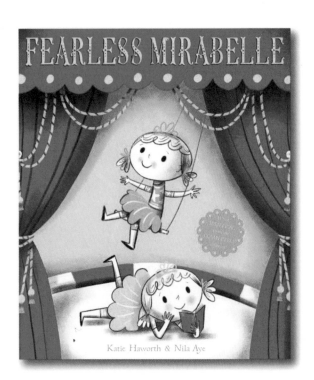

ISBN: 978-1-78741-073-2

ISBN: 978-1-78370-801-7